BIBBIT
JUMPS

Bei Lynn

BIBBIT JUMPS

Translated by Helen Wang

GECKO PRESS

Bibbit loved jumping
but not into water.

Anything but water.

"Come on, Bibbit,
you can do it!"

The frog pyramid

High, higher, higher!

Bibbit and his friends were building a pyramid beside the pond. They wanted to add a fifth level, so they could beat their own record.

They held each other tight and spread
their feet on the ground.

"Don't sneeze!" said Bibbit.

Then it was Bibbit's turn. He warmed
up for an enormous jump, rocking back
and forth, left and right, until the soles of
his feet felt like bouncy balls. That's the
time to jump! He sprang from the tips of
his toes—high enough for a sixth row,
a seventh even.

But he went too high and came down
head first like an arrow.

The pyramid split in two. Oops!

Bibbit's little sister was watching with her friends. She was just a tadpole. She wanted to try everything that Bibbit did.

Tadpoles can't jump or climb, so Bibbit tried to help them make a pyramid. But the tadpoles were as round as beads, and slippery.

A careless wriggle—and they all tumbled into the pond.

Bibbit jumped in to rescue them— forgetting he'd forgotten how to swim.

Tadpoles lose their tails when they become frogs. But when Bibbit was a tadpole and lost his tail, his new arms and legs didn't know what to do.

They still don't.

The tadpoles swam over and helped Bibbit to the bank. Instead of Bibbit rescuing the tadpoles, the tadpoles rescued him!

Learning to swim

Bibbit wanted to learn how to swim again.

"How could you have forgotten?" asked his friend Lulu. "You just pull with your hands, then kick with your legs!"

"No," said another frog. "It's the other
way around: you kick with your legs, then
pull with your hands!"

Bibbit's friends from the frog pyramid
all said different things. So they decided
to show him instead.

Splish!

"Got it?"

"No," said Bibbit.

Splash!

"Now do you see?"

"No," said Bibbit.

Splosh!

"How about that?"

"No!"

Splish! Splash! Splosh!

One by one, Bibbit's friends dived into the water. They all swam perfectly.

Even Huahua the squirrel, who was watching, could see how to do it.

"Come on, Bibbit. You can do it!"
said Lulu.

"I think I'm remembering," said
Bibbit. "My arms, my legs…my whole
body is remembering how to swim!"

Bibbit leapt down from the tree and
stood at the edge of the pond. He took a
deep breath, raised his arms, and cried,
"Watch me! I'm amazing!"

Bibbit actually was amazing. He leapt high, hugged his knees, and spun once, twice... He shut his eyes and thought of all the times he'd jumped higher or further than ever before, felt this rush of air on his face. It was thrilling. He loved this feeling!

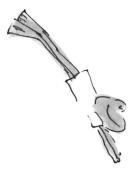

He remembered the time he jumped
so high that when he spread his toes
and flapped his arms, for a moment he
thought he'd turned into a bird.

And he remembered when he was a
tadpole, wiggle-dancing with the water
plants in the pond, and racing
with the other tadpoles to see
who could swim fastest.

Bibbit could hardly wait to be back in the water, swimming without a care in the world.

But there was no *Splash!*

Only voices crying, "No! No! Oh no!"

Oh dear. Bibbit still hadn't done it.

"It's impossible to swim," he said, "with so many frogs in the pond."

Picnic

Bibbit's little sister was no longer a tadpole. Now he called her Little Frog.

Even though it wasn't a birthday, Bibbit and Little Frog wanted to do something special.

When Bibbit woke up, he saw a note from Little Frog.

Picnic time! Follow the arrows.

Bibbit followed the arrows left, then right, then straight ahead. He saw a note on a mulberry tree:

Pick some fruit while you're here.

Bibbit picked some berries and kept following the arrows—right, right, straight ahead, left. Another note told him to go a little further, then turn left, then:

Pick a banana from the tree.

Bibbit looked up and saw a tree with a big bunch of bananas. He aimed for the highest one. It was harder to reach than he thought.

He kept trying, and each time he jumped, he caught the sweet smell of banana. How could he reach those delicious bananas?

Bibbit remembered his special technique. He jumped on the spot a few times, and when his feet felt like bouncy balls, he leapt as high as he could...but not high enough.

Bibbit didn't give up. He focused on the lowest, loveliest banana, the most fragrant banana in the bunch. He crouched way down low, then sprang way up high. He grabbed the banana. He pushed his feet on the bunch beside it, straightened his back and pulled and pulled.

Snap!

The banana smelled as sweet and fragrant as can be.

Bibbit carried it in his arms and kept following Little Frog's arrows.

The next note said:

Sit on this rock and think about things.

But Bibbit didn't want to sit and think.

He knew that if he stopped, he'd want to eat the banana...all of it.

He heard a voice saying, "Look!
A bouncing banana!"

Bibbit didn't stop to explain, he just
kept leaping, as fast as he could.

Boing, boing, boing!

The sun grew brighter and brighter.
And hotter and hotter. It felt too hot for
a picnic. If Bibbit had known how hot
it would be, he would have suggested to
Little Frog that they stay at home.

Then the arrows started to point back
to their garden.

Was the picnic finished?

Had he missed one of the arrows?
Had Little Frog drawn one pointing the
wrong way?

But there in the garden were Little
Frog and their friends were standing in
the garden, smiling and waving.

Was this her plan all along? Clever
Little Frog! Now they could enjoy a
picnic and stay at home—both at the
same time!

All the frogs came to the picnic.
They enjoyed the breeze and took
ice-cubes fresh from the kitchen.
Then they fell asleep on their pillows
under the tree.

Bibbit thought about how he had discovered a new thing to love, besides jumping: a picnic-at-home. As he smiled and munched the mulberries and the banana, a thought came to him.

"Little Frog," he said, "why did you make me walk all that way just to have a picnic at home?"

Little Rabbit's birthday

Bibbit had been growing flowers in a pot for Little Rabbit's birthday present. He'd planted the seeds in spring then watered them every day and waited.

Slowly, the seeds sprouted and grew and put out leaves, then more leaves. The leaves put out buds, then even more buds, and eventually—*pop*, *pop*, *pop*, *pop*—the buds opened! They were blue, star-shaped flowers.

Bibbit gave one to Little Frog.

As they walked to Little Rabbit's house, they kept meeting friends who admired the plant and Bibbit's green fingers.

Bibbit was so happy that he gave each friend a flower.

When they reached Little Rabbit's house, there was only one flower left in the pot.

"Shall I put my flower back?" asked Little Frog.

But it was too late. "It won't live," said Bibbit, wishing he'd had time to grow more.

Then he tripped over, and the last flower in the pot snapped off!

At the door, Little Rabbit looked at Little Frog and Bibbit, and the flower pot with no flowers.

Bibbit said sadly, "I planted a whole pot full of blue star flowers especially for you, but...now only the leaves are left."

Little Rabbit sat down beside Bibbit.

"I love leaves," he said.

He picked up the pot and peered at
the leaves. "Look! There are lots of blue
dots, twinkling like stars underneath!"

Bibbit looked closely, "They're buds,
just beginning to open."

"You really do have green fingers,"
said Little Rabbit. "Thank you, Bibbit, for
this wonderful present."

"And here's a present from me,"
said Little Frog, giving him her flower.
"Happy birthday, Little Rabbit!"

Not giving up

Thud! An apple fell to the ground.
It rolled down the hill, on and on,
until it ran into a haystack.

It was a very special apple, very sweet and very big—so big that Bibbit and his friends could see it in the distance and so sweet-smelling that anyone who came near longed for a bite.

The frogs decided to have a feast. One frog moved a little stone to sit on, another brought a ladder, and another climbed right to the top of the apple.

When everyone was there, and they could wait no longer, they tucked in. *Crunch... Crunch... Crunch...* It was so loud the grass quivered. They chomped with delight: *Chomp... Chomp... Chomp.*

Then the frogs started to grimace. "Pah!" They spat out bits of apple as their faces turned even greener than usual.

They ran away, shouting, "Yuk! Sour!"

"It's the most disgusting apple ever!" called Lulu as she bounced off.

Soon, everyone had gone.

Everyone except Bibbit and Little Frog.

Bibbit didn't want to go. He kept on eating, chewing each mouthful slowly

Little Frog didn't want any more, but she wouldn't go home without him.

Evening came, and Bibbit was still
eating. "I'm going to finish it all,"
he said, "I'm not going to give up."

"It's not a competition," said Little
Frog. She couldn't understand why he
was so determined. But Bibbit wasn't
giving up, so Little Frog stayed to keep
him company.

Time passed slowly. When the moon finally rose, Bibbit's belly was almost as round as the moon. He could hardly manage another bite, but still he said, "I'm going to finish it. I'm not giving up..."

"I'm ready to go home," said Little Frog. "But I'll stay with you. I'm not giving up either."

Jumping all day long

"One." *Bop.*

"Two." *Bop.*

"Three." *Bop.*

"Four—only four nuts left!" *Bop.*

Huahua the squirrel had been counting nuts, but someone kept knocking at the door! *Bop! Bop! Bop!*

But it wasn't knocking, it was Bibbit, trying out his jumps.

"Good morning, Huahua," said Bibbit. "Now that you've opened the door and I can see your friendly face, my jumping practice is going to be even more fun!"

Huahua was outside when her friend Jianjian arrived.

"I heard you only have four nuts left," said Jianjian. "I've come to help you pick some more."

"There's no need. Look, Bibbit has just picked all these. He said he wanted to try out jumping extra high."

"He must really love jumping."

"He truly does. But Jianjian, could you help me take them home?"

Bibbit was great at jumping—but not so good at carrying nuts home.

Jumping all day long again

Up in the bright blue sky was a little green bird with a twig of berries in its beak. The tiny red berries looked so pretty, and the closer Bibbit got, the brighter and sweeter they appeared.

What would they taste like? he
wondered. If they fell from the sky, would
they roll like marbles?

The little bird with the berries flew
slowly, slowly, soaring up, then
swooping down. It was helping Bibbit
with his jumping practice!

After the rain, the rainbow came.

Jump! Jump! Jump, jump, jump...jump!

Gentle bounces or big strong leaps, Bibbit loved them all. He jumped to touch violet three times, yellow five times and green twice. Each time he touched the rainbow, it wobbled.

Bibbit went on leaping until he'd touched indigo, orange, blue and red.

The rainbow couldn't help smiling. "Hey, that tickles, I can't take any more! See you next time, Bibbit!" And it disappeared over the horizon.

No jumping

"What's the matter?" asked Little Frog.
"Why are you under so many covers?
Have you caught a cold?"

Bibbit's eyes looked dull. He shook
his head.

"You haven't jumped at all today," said Little Frog. "You haven't even moved. Do your feet hurt?"

Bibbit shook his head again. "I do feel a little hot," he said eventually.

Little Frog went to open the window to let in some air, but the air blew the leaves off Bibbit. Well, not all of them. There were so many.

"What is it, Bibbit? What's wrong with you?"

"Little Frog, don't you think I look like a mummy?"

Bibbit hadn't answered Little Frog's question. He wasn't ill at all. He was doing an experiment. If he saved up a whole day of jumping, would he be able to jump higher and further the following day?

Bibbit might have spent the entire day without jumping, but his mind was filled with high bounces, long leaps, and all kinds of beautiful arcing jumps.

An adventure

Bibbit and Little Frog were sitting in
a tree chatting with a little green bird.
How far is far away? wondered Little Frog.

How much do you have to dream about
something for it to be called a dream?
wondered Bibbit.

The little green bird said she once flew for a whole week to a mountain with delicious fruits and nuts, but it was very far, and she had to stop at several cities on the way.

Bibbit and Little Frog were curious.

"Are cities fun?" asked Bibbit. "Are the trees there taller than the trees here?"

The bird told them there are very tall trees in the city, and buildings even taller than the trees. When you stand on top of those buildings, you see a very long way into the distance.

"Do you think I could jump onto a tall building?" Bibbit wanted to know.

"The buildings are very high. I often see people standing on top, but I don't know how they get there," said the little green bird.

But before she flew off, she told them, "If you follow this river, it'll take you to a city."

"Let's go, Bibbit!" said Little Frog.

Bibbit rolled his eyes. His mouth opened and closed, but no words came out.

"We were just wondering if it was fun in the city, weren't we?" said Little Frog.

But what if we get lost? What if we get hungry? What if we can't get back? Bibbit didn't ask the questions out loud, but they were bouncing about inside his head. He wasn't brave enough to go the city.

The next morning, he found a note:

Gone to see the city—
that's my dream for the day.

Little Frog had gone.

Bibbit wanted to see the city too, but when he looked at the river his legs turned to jelly. What if Little Frog got lost? What if she got hungry? What if she couldn't find her way back... What then?

He shouted into the distance, "Little Frog! I'm coming to rescue you!"

"Take my boat," said Huahua.

"Don't be scared! Just be careful!"
said Jianjian.

Is it possible not to be scared? Bibbit
wondered.

Luckily, the river wasn't flowing fast,
and the little boat didn't rock too much
as he set off on his city adventure.

The journey went smoothly.

After a while, the air on his skin felt
different. He must have arrived.

"Little Frog, I'm coming. Wait for me!"
he cried.

Bibbit noticed a little red man.

"Have you seen my sister Little Frog?"
he asked.

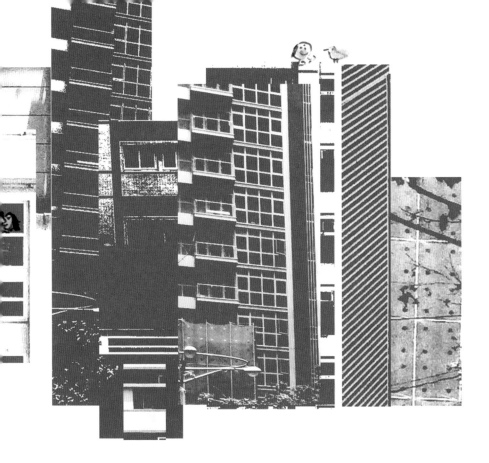

The little red man said nothing.

And then he disappeared.

In his place was a little green man.

"Have you seen my sister Little Frog?" asked Bibbit.

The little green man said nothing either. He just kept on walking, faster and faster.

"Why are you ignoring me?" Bibbit asked.

"He's working, he's busy," said a voice. "But I'm free. My name's Bruno."

Bibbit looked at Bruno, who was the same orange as Little Frog, and told him the whole story: about the little green bird, about Little Frog's note, about his friends, the boat, and the river.

"I guess she's gone to find a tall building," said Bibbit.

"A tall building..." said Bruno. "Let's go and look for her together."

Bruno took him around the city.
Bibbit never imagined there could
be so many tall buildings!

They walked for a long time.
Eventually, a particular building
caught his eye.

"This building is orange like Little Frog. I think she'll be at the top of this one," said Bibbit. "But I'll never be able to jump that high."

"We'll take the easy way," said Bruno.

He led Bibbit through the main doors of the building, then through a smaller door, which closed behind them. He stood and stared at all the buttons.

"I can't reach," said Bruno.

"I can!" said Bibbit, jumping up.

Bruno told him which button.

It was easy for Bibbit. As soon as he pressed it, he thought he heard rumbling. But he couldn't be sure. He thought the little room might be moving. But how could they get to the top of the building by standing in a tiny room?

There were lots of things in the city that Bibbit didn't understand, so he waited patiently to see what would happen.

There was a *ping* and the door opened.

"Little Frog!"

"Bibbit!" Little Frog leapt over and gave her brother a big hug, "I knew you would come!"

They stood in the moonlight on top of the tall building. Far in the distance, they could see a mountain.

"Do you think that's where home is?" asked Little Frog.

The moon leaned close.

"Yes, that's your home."

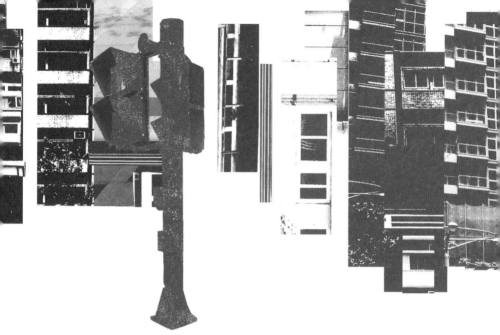

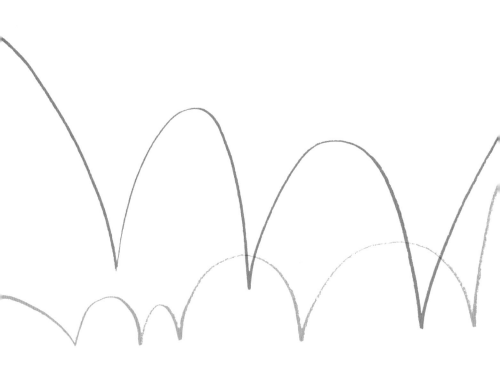

This edition first published in 2020 by Gecko Press
PO Box 9335, Wellington 6141, New Zealand
info@geckopress.com

English-language edition © Gecko Press Ltd 2020
Translation © Helen Wang 2020

Text and illustrations by Bei Lynn © 2018
Published by arrangement with Walkers Cultural Co., Ltd/Pace Books
through Bardon-Chinese Media Agency
All rights reserved

Distributed in the United States and Canada by Lerner Publishing Group, lernerbooks.com
Distributed in the United Kingdom by Bounce Sales and Marketing, bouncemarketing.co.uk
Distributed in Australia and New Zealand by Walker Books Australia, walkerbooks.com.au

Sponsored by Ministry of Culture, Republic of China (Taiwan)

Edited by Penelope Todd
Design and typesetting by Vida Kelly
Printed in China by Everbest Printing Co. Ltd,
an accredited ISO 14001 & FSC-certified printer

ISBN hardback: 978-1-776572-77-9 (USA)
ISBN paperback: 978-1-776572-78-6
Ebook available

For more curiously good books, visit geckopress.com